Teaching with the Fables
A Holistic Approach

written & illustrated by
Sieglinde De Francesca

third edition ◆ revised

(teach wonderment)

also by
Sieglinde De Francesca

Coloring with Block Crayons,
a manual of coloring techniques for teaching to young children

A Donsy of Gnomes
7 gentle gnome stories & more

The Tales of Limindoor Woods
a series of chapter books

The Way of Gnome – book 1
Gnomes & Friends – book 2
The Gnomes' Rosette – book 3
Nine Gnome Nights – books 4

11 Downloadable Children's Stories
and toy patterns to go with them
kitntales.com

First Edition 2007
Second Edition 2013 ◆ Revised
Third Edition 2019 ◆ Revised

teachwonderment.com
ISBN 978-1-60461-621-7

Introduction

"A story, a story, please, tell me a story!"

What a fine thing for any child, a story to dream with, a story to learn with, a story to grow with. The world's treasury of fairy tales, folk tales, fables and myths, is a rich legacy for all children.

By understanding how the evolution of human consciousness is reflected in the evolution of the individual child, you can see how this progression of stories maps a wisdom path that nourishes the child's very being.

There is a gentle awakening as the child moves from the dream-like world of fairy tales to the humorous, self-revealing world of the fables. The veiled world of magic, of archetypes, of 'happily ever after', gradually lifts to expose the world of the individual, a self, separate from the archetype.

At around age 8, or when the child is in second grade, is the time for the child to hear stories that reveal the human moral contest between right and wrong. There are saint and hero stories of humans who have striven to do good; to be kind, brave and generous. Conversely, there are stories that reflect the baser side of human nature, human shortcomings that include; pride, foolishness, selfishness and laziness. These are the fables.

More often than not, the characters of these stories who reveal these behaviors are animals; animals who can be laughed at, animals whose human-like antics delight and ultimately, teach.

The fables we are most familiar with are attributed to Aesop, a Greek slave who lived about 550 BC. There is little that is really known of his life. Elements of many of the fables are found in the Indian Jataka tales, or Buddha's birth stories of his previous incarnations. Over time, many such tales from various sources were come to be known as Aesopic fables, and over time each of the simple tales was given a "set moral" to sum up its teaching.

This book offers what may be, for many, a new approach to teaching the fables. You will discover how to expand a short fable into an imaginative story, or fable story, that is interesting and alive with meaning, and offers a far deeper learning experience.

Besides working with the nurturing, moral aspects of the stories, you will learn how the fables can be used to teach the language arts, including creative writing and poetry, animal studies, and, in some cases, simple natural science lessons. You can also awaken the child's sense of wonderment as you explore how to render these stories into various forms of expression, such as drawing, painting, modeling, puppetry and theater.

In short, you are offered a formula, or approach, to manifesting a broad, fun, creative, integrated lesson plan around a relatively simple subject. This formula, you may find, can be easily applied to other subjects you wish to offer to your children. With it, you will enjoy bringing the fables, and all other courses, to life in a magical and nourishing way.

Like a seed, something as "small" as a fable can grow to great import. Or, as one moral from Aesop's fable *The Lion and the Mouse* says ...

"Little friends may prove to be great friends."

TABLE of CONTENTS

Part 1   Teaching with the fables in a living way

The Fable

Every interaction that you have with a child, in some way teaches that child. Young children learn through imitation, but also through an awakened imagination. Whether you are simply spending time with your child, or teaching a prepared lesson, that interaction gives you the opportunity to open up worlds of wonder to your child. And what better way to do that than with a story? The expanded fable story is a particularly rich medium to teach with.

Of the numerous fables that are written by Aesop, or included in the Aesopic genre, most have animals as the main characters, and all have morals that have been attributed to them. These maxims, or lessons, relate to specific human traits that are illustrated by the animal's behavior.

These stories have been used as teaching tools for hundreds of years, usually with the moral recited at the end of each telling, leaving little room for personal interpretation. Imagine the benefit though in allowing the child to discover the fable's real message by using their own powers of perception, instead of learning only one, pre-established or pre-conveyed moral per fable.

The Expanded Fable Story

In order to really nourish the child with the fables, these stories must be offered in a living way. The collection of simple, short animal tales with their locked and limited messages can be transformed into a wholesome body of enjoyable narratives, rich with significance. These are *expanded* fable stories.

The expanded fable story adds to the learning experience in that it offers a broad groundwork of factual information about the animal and its habitat. This enrichment can enliven and deepen the child's experience of the story and further their grasp of the tale's intrinsic message.

In order to expand the fable into a fable story, you need to first find out what you can about the characters, the setting, and the events of the tale. Though most of Aesop's characters are animals, some are people and a few are simply plants or the elements.

If the fable you choose is an animal tale, it will be important to familiarize yourself with all that you can know about the animal. What is it that makes that particular animal distinctive? What are its strengths and its weaknesses? How does it live? What is it about the animal's behavior that reveals the moral message of the fable?

What is there to know about the setting for the story? Is it significant to the outcome of the story? What are the events that take place? What is it about those events that carry the intended message of the tale?

Researching the characters

You can expand the fable into a fascinating nature lesson by including a wealth of information about the different animal characters. Research all that you can about each animal.

- Try to observe the animal in its natural habitat. Touch it, if possible.
- What descriptive words would you attribute to the animal: its color, size, texture, sound, smell?
- How would you describe this animal to someone who has never seen one?
- How would you draw this animal?
- How does this animal move?
- What and how does it eat?
- What is the animal's habitat?
- What is the animal's distinctive behavior?
- What are the animal's strengths and weaknesses?
- What is one remarkable thing about the animal?
- What temperament would you say the animal has?
   Is it flighty and fidgety? Is it slow and phlegmatic?
   Is it fierce and dynamic? Is it timid and shy?

If the characters are human, what can you surmise about each one? Granted, most fables give little information about the people in them, but with a little imagination you can fill out the character to make him or her seem real.

- Who do you think this person is?
- What is the character's age?
- What is the character's work?
- What is the character's temperament?
   Is it flighty and fidgety? Is it slow and phlegmatic?
   Is it fierce and dynamic? Is it timid and shy?
- Is the character wise or foolish?
- Is he likeable or disagreeable?
- What descriptive words would you attribute to this person: colors, textures, sounds, size?
- How would you draw this person?

Defining the story's setting

Enhance the nature lesson aspect of the fable by including information about the animal's habitat. What you can tell about the setting of the story and how is it significant to the events that take place? The clearer picture you have in your mind of the place, the more effective will be your telling of the tale.

- How important is the setting to the story?
- Could the story take place in another location? Where would that be?
- Can you compare it to some place the child knows?
- What is the terrain like?
- What is the vegetation like?
- What is the weather like?
- What is the time of day? Is this significant?
- What is the season? Is this significant?
- What words you can use to describe the setting: color, texture, light, smells, and temperature?

The moral message

All Aesopic tales, in their simplicity, reveal some aspect of human behavior. At some point in history each fable was given a set moral to sum up the lesson to be learned from that behavior. Sometimes, there are multiple morals attributed to a single fable.

When choosing a fable, ask yourself what is the lesson you wish to teach your child? There are some fables with positive directives that support right action, and some that reveal human foibles and the folly of making poor choices. Please visit the Appendix on page 53.

In the positive vein, some fables support:
- Sticking to one's purpose: *Wolf and the Kid*
- Using one's wits: *The Crow and the Pitcher*
- Finding strength in unity: *The Bundle of Sticks*

Whereas, some reveal human vices such as:
- Greed: *The Dog and his Reflection*
- Self deception: *The Fox and the Grapes*
- Stubbornness: *The Two Goats*
- Anger: *The Bear and the Bees*

Some fables offer positive messages, while also revealing less desirable human behavior. For example, *The Hare and the Tortoise*, illustrates the benefit of sticking to one's purpose, it also reveals the folly of pride and being too sure of oneself.

How to Expand the fable

With any story, the questions "*who, what, where, when*, and *how*" must be answered. A story should have an introduction, some form of crisis and a resolution. A fable, though sparse in content, already contains the essential *crisis* and *resolution*. By expanding the context of a fable, the picture of the characters and settings are enhanced, making the whole more substantial, interesting and engaging.

It is primarily the part of the story that introduces the characters and setting of the tale that is expanded. Instead of starting with, "Once, when a lion was asleep a little mouse began running up and down upon him," Aesop's *The Lion and the Mouse* (as the fable does) you would introduce the story with a description of the setting, and create a fuller characterization of the animal.

For example, when you do your research for the fable of *The Lion and the Mouse*, you will learn how lions and mice live in open woodlands and thick bush, scrub, and tall grassy areas; areas that are rich with game for the lions, and with grass seeds for the mice.

You will learn how the lion's tawny colored fur makes it easy to hide; how lions are fierce predators, and will eat anything from an elephant to a mouse, and, sadly, because they are predators, how they are highly valued by hunters.

When researching mice you will likely learn how mice rely on their size, speed, and ingenuity to survive, and have been know to think out a strategy before doing something, how they eat almost anything and are great nibblers, being not afraid to try new foods.

All of these facts are interesting and can be relevant to the expansion of the short fable. When you start to create your characterizations you will want to weave in this information, making the characters real and interesting.

When you introduce the characters, describe where and how they live. Keep in mind the message of the fable. In the case of *The Lion and the Mouse*, we see how proud and mighty the lion is and how he is humbled by being saved by the mouse. We see how though the mouse is small; it is still capable of rescuing the great lion. Our expansion of the story will focus on the contrasts between the two animals.

You might start the fable with:

> "*The sun glared down on the vast open grasslands. Waves of shimmering heat hung over the day. There was not a sound, nothing stirred, no flies buzzed, or grasshopper sawed. All were too hot.*
> *There, under a straggly old tree, that was all but bare of leaves, lay a great lion. Though massive and grand, known by all as the King of the Beasts, he could hardly be seen as he lay there so still, his tawny coat the color of the sun dried grasses. He slept.*"

Add as much as you feel is interesting and relevant to the story. The complete expanded version of *The Lion and the Mouse* is found on page 34.

When you describe elements of your story, speak to the listener's senses. Be sure to consider the following.

1.   Color: Bring as much adjective color into your descriptions as possible and make the colors come alive. Even if the child does not know what a particular color is, he may learn through sound and association.
     - Tawny gold
     - Singing emerald
     - Silvery taupe grey
     - Calm azure
     - Flaming crimson

2.   Texture: Again, use interesting words, words that will grab their attention and make what you are describing seem real, almost tactile.
     - Prickly
     - Raspy
     - Velvety
     - Feathery
     - Wispy
     - Crackly
     - Jagged
     - Satiny
     - Creamy

3.   Sound: We are always learning from the sounds in our environment, but we rarely consciously listen. By including sound words another sense is awakened.
     - Whispery
     - Crackly
     - Snappy
     - Scratching
     - Thundering
     - Bellowing
     - Crunching
     - Nibbling
     - Rustling
     - Purring

4.   Smells: Scent is one of the senses that we pay so little attention to, unless we experience a new or intense smell. But by incorporating scents into your story the setting and events will become more vivid.
     - Spicy
     - Green
     - Sharp
     - Sweet
     - Clean
     - Musky
     - Damp
     - Fresh
     - Dusty
     - Acrid

5. Temperature: Our sense of temperature is important to our comfort and survival. Describing something's temperature will make the experience of it more real.

- Roasting
- Biting
- Sweltering
- Clammy

- Gently mild
- Sizzling
- Prickly cold
- Burning

6. Movement: Words that add movement, add life to your characters.

- Pounce
- Skitter
- Slither
- Wave
- Sweep
- Dance
- Pulse

- Flicker
- Explode
- Twitch
- Creep
- Thrash
- Wiggle
- Roil

After you have introduced and described the characters and the setting, including much pertinent and interesting information about them, you will want to start to tell the events of the actual fable.

In *The Lion and the Mouse*, the fable tells of the lion catching and releasing a mouse, and how the mouse later saves the lion. It is a simple story, but if you have made the scene vivid with good descriptive words and relevant information the story will come alive and end up teaching so much more than the bare bones fable (found on page 32).

It is very important that the moral message of the fable be revealed through the enhancement of the material. There should be no need to limit the child's perception of the story's message by reciting a *locked or "set moral"* at the end. The listener should be able to discover the story's significance through the development of the characters, the language and the manner that the story is told.

Teaching the Whole Child

Head, Heart & Hand

With a holistic education one seeks to educate the whole child. To teach the whole child we must teach to the child's *head, heart* and *hand* in equal measure and in an integrated way. We teach to the intellect, the thinking *head* with academics; the feeling, expressive *heart* with the arts; and the active will of the *hand* with physical, practical activities. Yet, when the lesson is academic, we imbue it with activities of the *heart* and *hand*. When it is an art, or *heart* lesson, we include *head* and *hand* elements, and so forth.

In the matter of teaching the fables, the head part of the lesson is the information given in the story. The heart aspect is, in part, the emotional response to the story and the impulse to respond to that response with an artistic rendering. The hand part of the lesson is met in any physical activity that comes out of the lesson. Just as the head, heart and hand are parts of a being, so too these three aspects of the lesson are integrated parts of a whole.

The Rhythm, Reverence and Ritual

Rhythm, Reverence and Ritual, the new 'three R's', are essential elements of a heartfelt lesson plan. A healthy, rhythmic lesson breathes with an alternating inward and outward focus.

The *in breath* of academic studies might move to the *out breath* of some of the artistic activities, to return again to the academic in fresh way, only to then move to the *out breath* of a physical activity, and so on. In this manner the whole child engages with the lesson in a living, breathing way.

The sense of reverence is evident in the way the lesson is prepared and presented. The care and attention one gives to the lesson materials, reflects the respect that is felt for the study and the student. Inspiration, creativity, appropriateness, thoroughness and caring are essential elements of a reverently created lesson.

Ritual, as in 'custom' or 'habit,' is a key element of a vital lesson. Rituals are events experienced in a recurring manner, such as: a verse that is repeated daily, and a dependable, set structure to the way the whole lesson is formed. Other rituals may include: how the story is told each day, where you and your child sit, if a bell is rung, a candle lit, and which verses are told at the story's beginning and end.

Storytelling or "Telling the Story"

Since the fables are brought to the children orally, they should be told in an effective and engaging manner. Many people feel insecure about telling stories, believing that storytelling is an art that requires special skills, but this is not necessarily the case.

First and foremost, remember that when you tell a story you are *giving a gift*. True gifts come from the heart and are prepared with care.

With preparation and practice, by keeping an open mind, and by engaging in the guidelines below, you can strengthen your storytelling abilities. You will also be giving your child the valuable experience of watching how you learn and grow.

There are really only a few things to remember when you tell a story.

1. Familiarize yourself with the story. Know all that you can about the characters, setting and events. By being able to visualize all of the elements of the story, you will better be able to bring them to life in the telling. Tell the story over and over to yourself, including all of the details. Outline it in your mind. What are the key words and images? Tell the story to yourself and visualize telling it to the child.

2. Try to get a sense of the listener's temperament. Is it sanguine, phlegmatic, choleric or melancholy, or a combination of these?
   - A *sanguine* child is generally optimistic, cheerful, impulsive, possibly acting on whims and often unpredictable. Think of the butterfly, flitting from place to place.
   - The *choleric* is a doer and a leader, ambitious and energetic, sometimes easily angered.
   - A *phlegmatic* person is calm, consistent and steady, and often delights in eating.
   - The *melancholic* is thoughtful, kind and considerate, highly creative and sometimes sad or depressed.

   You may wish to match the tone or temperament of your story to that of the listener.

3. What mood is evoked by the message of the story? Is it amusing or dramatic? Mood can be conveyed by the quality and rhythm of your voice, the descriptions of the story's characters and settings, and by the manner you unravel the events. Be careful, though, not to overly dramatize the telling.

4. Always leave room for the child to discover the spirit of the story. If the fable is amusing, as many of the fables are, let the humor come through in the telling. Laughter is a wonderful thing, and will greatly contribute to the child's enjoyment of the story.

5. Fables are a form of nature tales. Communicate your reverence for the sacredness of all life by letting awe, wonder and love come through in your voice and your manner of telling the story.

6. How will you begin and end your story? A fable can still, like a fairy tale, start with "Once upon a time," or "There was once…" However, though it won't end with "they all lived happily ever after," you may wish to come up with a closing that you use for all your fables.

7.   Establish the right environment and procedures to create a supportive mood for your storytelling. Perhaps you will have a special story chair, and next to it a small table decorated with a candle and/or flowers, or perhaps beeswax figures of the animal characters. To avoid having the child easily distracted, have him face in the least busy direction in the room, and make sure that you don't have a bright light or window behind you, so your face can be easily seen.

8.   You may want to create a storytelling ritual. This could include lighting a candle, singing a song or ringing a chime. You may put on a story shawl or cover the story chair with a special spread. You may have set verses to start and end your stories. When lighting the candle you might use the following song/verse.

> *Our candle shines so brightly,*
> *It cheers us with its light.*
> *We love to see it glowing.*
> *It's such a lovely sight.*

When the story is over, you might finish with;

> *Stars and moon and sun, now my story's done.*

or,

> *That is the telling of that tale,*
> *May it now rest in our hearts.*

9.   Maintain eye contact with the child as you relate the story. You can also use some hand gestures. But, refrain from over dramatizing the story. The story itself, the language you use, and the mood in which the story is told should be sufficient.

10. You may find it helpful to remind the child the following thoughts, as necessary;

> *"The story needs quiet to be told."*
> *"Please sit on your sitting place, turtles sit on their tummies."*
> *"We will put the story aside now, until all is quiet"*
> *"If you have heard this story before, remember that it is like meeting with an old friend.*
> *Sometimes our friends change. But we still meet them with a smile."*

11. Most importantly, relax; remember that you are giving the child a very special gift. Above all, enjoy yourself.

Creating the Lesson Plan

If you wish to fully explore the extent of teaching possibilities presented by each fable story it is important to create a lesson plan, regardless if you are home schooling or classroom teaching.

In order to teach to the whole child, we see that there are several essential elements to creating a living lesson.

- Teach to the head, heart and hand
- Create an organic rhythm in the lesson
- Convey a sense of reverence
- Include ritual in the lesson
- Review work from the previous lesson
- Introduce new material
- Render the material in an artistic medium

Lesson Plan Outline

With these elements in mind, you can teach your child with the fables using an integrated plan to insure a holistic learning experience. What follows is an outline to use as a guideline. Although at first it may seem complex, after you have taught the fables using this outline for a while, you will find the elements of it that work for you. Do remember to keep a breath-like flow to the different parts of your lessons, and *do not plan to do too much*! *Quality*, as always, is more important than *quantity* when preparing lessons.

a) Make preparations
   i) Choose a block, or series, of fables to teach
   ii) Choose a specific fable to start with
   iii) Research and take creative time to expand the fable story
   iv) Plan out the rest of the lesson

b) Review the previous fable (before introducing a new one)
   i) You, or the child, will retell the fable story, or significant aspects of it
   ii) Child re-reads writing in Main Lesson book (optional)
   iii) Child recites poem (optional)

c) Fable story
   i) Create the storytelling environment
   ii) Tell the extended fable
   iii) Introduce fable poem (optional)

d) Main Lesson book work
   i) Review previous work (optional)
   ii) Write text in book
   iii) Read text in book
   iv) Draw/ or paint an illustration

e)	Do an additional rendering of the fable (optional)	f)	Special activities (optional)
	i) Prepare materials		i) Schedule activity
	ii) Give example/ instructions		ii) Prepare for activity
	iii) Complete the rendering		iii) Give example/ instructions
			iv) Complete the activity

Preparations

When it comes to preparing your lessons, it is good to remember that you really need only teach *one new thing* to your child per day. Teaching in this way is about inspiring your child, not filling your child with information.

When teaching the fables, what is your main objective? Will you use the fables as a language arts lesson, or a nature study, or both? Are you choosing your fables around a particular theme, perhaps a particular moral message, or particular kinds of animals? Are the fables humorous or serious? How many fables do you plan on bringing to your child? How many a week? (One or two is recommended.)

You will need to prepare for the rest of the lesson as well. How will you review the lesson from the day before? How do you plan on telling the fable story? How much time will be spent with the Main Lesson book and what do you want the work to include? Will there be another separate artistic rendering, and if so, what? These are all questions that you will need to answer before you can start planning you lesson.

Choosing Which Fables to Teach

Whether you plan to teach the fables throughout the year, or in blocks of several weeks, you will need to decide how many you will present. You will want to choose the fables carefully. There are so many of Aesop's fables to choose from. When creating your lesson plan for a block of lessons on the fables, you may wish to group the fables in a particular manner. The fables can be categorized in any number of ways.

- By moral message
- By character (animal and/or human)
- By the manner you wish to illustrate the story (drawing or painting)
- By the medium you wish to use to render the story
- By the natural science lesson related to the story

A chart categorizing a number of favorite fables can be found in the Appendix on page 53. Choose your fables well. Although they are simple, they can be very powerful. Teaching more fables is not necessarily better than teaching a carefully chosen few in a holistic way.

The Review

The review is important because learning is not something that happens only in the classroom. The child has had at least 24 hours for material learned the previous day to 'cook' in the subconscious. When asked to recall a previous lesson, one that has been taught in a living way, the child experiences a deepening of that learning. This part of the lesson plan naturally precedes the offering of new material.

The daily review of previous work is an important ritual for the child. In the case of your teaching with the fables, you may have the child repeat the expanded fable story from the earlier lesson, or ask them to prompt you as you repeat it. You might also retell the fable from another perspective, for example as if you were one of the animals telling the story from their particular, unique viewpoint.

Before moving on to the new material, you may also wish to review the Main Lesson book work that was done. Reread the text that was written and use the opportunity to do some Language Arts exercises. Some suggestions of these exercises are found on page 19. You may also wish to discuss the illustration the child did. Point out aspects of the drawing or painting that were successful and ask the child where there may be room for improvement.

The review time is also the time when the child can recite a poem learned in the previous lesson. This activity helps enliven the memory and therefore deepens the learning of that lesson.

New material

The new material presented to the child need not be extensive, but every lesson should contain at least one *new idea*. In the case of the fables, it could be a deeper inquiry into the previously told fable, or perhaps more information about one of the animals, or the exploration of one of the natural science exercises. Or, it could be a new story. It is the way that the lesson is introduced that is important. Certainly the material that is offered should meet the child's level of development and be offered in a sensitive and engaging way.

Recording the Fable in the Main Lesson Book

The use of the Main Lesson Book is unique to the Waldorf curriculum. The book is a place where the child, by recording their lessons, creates a handmade text book that becomes a record of the process of their learning and striving.

The book should always be treated with respect and handled as if it were a special thing. Encourage the child to take time with the work they do. Remind them to clean their hands before working, and to use a drawing pad under their book.

The work in their Fable Main Lesson book will include writing, reading and drawing, all which will be related to the fable story. Decide if you will want a special cover and title page. Also, decide how the work will be laid out in the book and if there will be borders on the pages. Numbering the pages will help keep the work orderly. You might wish to make a mockup book as a reference before guiding your child to work in theirs.

◆   The Written Text

  As the writing done in the Main Lesson book is an aspect of Language Arts studies, you will want to pay quite a bit of attention to your preparations of this part of the work. The text you choose to have the child copy will have a multifold purpose. Not only will you be retelling, or paraphrasing the fable, but you will be choosing words that the child will be working with for their reading, spelling and writing lessons.

  Choose your text carefully; keeping in mind that less is more. You know how much time your child needs to write a certain amount of text. Generally one page will be adequate. Choose familiar words and/or words that are similar to familiar words, as well as new, challenging words.

  An example of a text that a child might write for *The Lion and the Mouse* might be as simple as:

  "Once a lion caught a mouse but then spared it. Later, hunters trapped the lion in a net. The mouse came and nibbled on the ropes and saved the lion."

  When you feel the child is ready to copy the text into the Main Lesson book be sure that he is on the correct page and that he knows about keeping a space, or margin, around what is written. Will you have the child write on a blank page, will there be borders, will there be bands of color to write on to keep the lines straight? Some feel that liners, a lined page slipped under the page to be written on, make for neat writing. But isn't it far better for the child to strive to control the neatness of his lines without a liner, even if it means making some mistakes?

  Be sure to teach the child creative ways to correct mistakes, as words may invariably be misspelled, misplaced or omitted. Also be sure to give adequate time for copy work, so the child feels no sense of pressure to finish.

  This is a time to pay close attention to the child's handwriting. Do offer guidance and correction so that he will be able to form his letters clearly and neatly. Have the child look at the overall appearance of his writing and locate which words are the most neat, legible and attractive.

  Ideally, the copy work should be written with thick colored pencils. Some teachers prefer the use of stick crayons. In no case should any writing be done with block crayons. Thin graphite pencils are not recommended at this developmental stage. The manner in which the child learns to grip his pencil when learning to write can affect his handwriting in the future.

  After writing the text in the Main Lesson book, there are several games you can play using the text on the board that will deepen its value in teaching reading and spelling.

1. After reading and rereading the text, have the child turn his back to the board. Ask: "Which words begin with B?" "Which words have two O's in them?" and similar questions.
2. While his back is turned, erase several key words. Have him look and see if he knows what words are missing. Can he come up and write them in?
3. Have a child come up and underline words that have certain sounds in them like the 'th' sound, or a long or short vowel, or any words that rhyme with each other.
4. Have him turn his back while you change the spelling of a few words. When he turns back you can ask if there is anything wrong, or you can tell him that there are 3 or 5 mistakes. "Can you spot them?"

5. Give the child a small note pad to notate any new words, his very own 'word book'. You might want to use these words later in an oral spelling quiz. It is fine if the text is still on the board and the child finds the word there. There is still memory and recognition at work.
6. Ask the child to compose a new sentence using some of the words that are on the board, or with certain words that have been underlined.

Clearly you would not play all of the games with each block of text, but certainly you can see how each will intensify the child's familiarity with the material.

You might like the creative writing to be a joint effort, in which case the child would work together with you, or other children, in writing out the story, and helping each other with the spelling, grammar and syntax. After you have checked the work, discussed it with the child or children, and corrected it, it can then be rewritten in the Main Lesson book.

Eventually you may decide that it is time for the writing in the Main Lesson book to be a creative writing exercise. If that is the case the child should be at the point where, when given a series of key words, he could write a series of sentences to retell the story in his own words. Perhaps this would be first written on a separate page, and later copied into their book.

◆ The Illustration

By illustrating a story the child learns to express himself in another medium. He will be able to communicate what he sees in his imagination, the images inspired by the story. This is a very empowering process. This is achieved by first learning a *vocabulary of expression*, techniques that you, the teacher, will teach him. With this vocabulary he will gain the tools to express his own imagination, his own inner vision.

Block crayons are the ideal medium for illustrating the fables in the Main Lesson book. Their shape allows for a versatility of stroke and gesture, and the colors that arise from using only the three primaries radiantly extend through the whole spectrum. Please note some primary color crayon illustrations of the fables can be seen starting on page 59.

Before you try to guide your child in drawing the characters of the fables, you will first want become familiar with the medium yourself. Practice the different strokes; drawing clouds, bands and ribbons with the three different sides of the blocks. To your child, you may wish to refer to the three sides of the crayons as Papa Bear (L), Mama Bear (M), and Baby Bear (S).

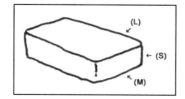 

Use the primary colors (carmine red, lemon yellow and ultramarine blue) and practice mixing the colors by drawing color circles and rainbows. There is a vitality that arises from blending the primaries that is not achieved with the locked secondary colors.

Be sure to have some sort of padding under your paper or book, either a drawing pad made of ten or more sheets of newsprint sandwiched between packing paper and taped around the edges with packing tape, or a sheet of smooth, vinyl faux leather that has a slightly padded backing. These can be made from yardage purchased at upholstery fabric stores.

When commencing a drawing, it is always best to indicate the 'ground line' with a band of yellow on which your figures will stand. This reminds us of the relationship between living things and the earth, and helps to orient the elements of the drawing.

Remember to blend your colors in a lively way and, very importantly, remember that you should always work with a light stroke. You can always make your colors more intense, but there is really no way to make them lighter.

When drawing an animal you can best capture its gesture by first discovering the line its spine makes. After the spine is drawn with the band or ribbon stroke, the mass of the body is indicated with cloud or band strokes. This is not a matter of outlining and filling in the shape. Always remember you need only to give a sense of the animal, its mood, gesture and strengths, without having to be anatomically precise. Try to capture those aspects of the animal that make it unique.

When drawing humans you need only make a small oval cloud shape for the head and draw a (medium side) band down from the head for the trunk. Draw two bands down for trousers, or just continue the band down for a dress. Smaller, curved strokes will make the arms and hands. No face will be needed and you need only suggest the hair.

You can draw the characters from the fable with a colored atmosphere around them, or you may wish to draw a scene with the characters in a landscape. If drawing just the character, variegate the color intensity of the atmosphere around it and take the color beyond the edges of the paper.

If drawing a landscape, you will want to first imagine the picture, where everything will go. Landscapes are generally drawn as if layered, starting from the furthest distance, the sky at the top of the page, down to the immediate foreground at the bottom of the page. Plan ahead where you will place the animals or story characters.

Plant life of course, will bring in another element to your images. Trees are drawn as they grow. 'Plant' a seed in the ground by drawing a light dot where the tree will stand. Then draw upward from that point. When you draw for your child, say, "See, I plant the seed here and it grows *up*!"

Be sure to always mix the colors to create lively hues, often going over most of a finished picture with a veil of yellow to enrich and brighten the colors. Keep your images simple and somewhat impressionistic.

Before you have the child draw in the Main Lesson book, you should be clear where the picture will go in the book, its orientation, whether or not there will be a border around the image, and what the content of the picture will be.

Some Main Lesson books have a piece of onion skin bound between the pages. This is to protect the images and text from marking each other. If your book does not have this you can give the child sheets of tracing paper to insert between the pages, as needed.

If you want the child to draw a frame around the Main Lesson book illustrations, this should be done first. Some frames can be drawn with a careful straight band, medium side of the block crayon. Children also enjoy creating borders of simple Form Drawing running motifs. Encourage the child to take time and care when creating the border, whatever style he chooses.

As the teacher you should have already done a sample drawing before guiding the child to draw the picture. This way you will be clear how to 'build' the image, and aware of any challenges the child may encounter when copying the picture.

Additional ways to render the Fable

To teach to the integrated *head, heart and hand* of the child, the intellectual activity of processing the new material (the story) is balanced with the artistic activity of rendering it into some form of creative expression.

The more mediums your child learns to render in, the more capable your child will become in communicating through those mediums. Besides the Main Lesson book drawings, you may have your child do a series of paintings of the fables, over a period of several weeks. Or, you may choose to alternate between several other forms of expression, such as modeling, puppetry or poetry.

If you have a time established to write and draw in your Main Lesson book, and still wish to explore another medium, do be aware of the rhythm of the lesson. Insert an 'in breath' activity such as writing or reading, between the 'out breath' of an artistic activity.

In your mind, go through all of the steps required of the art activity. Be sure to have all of the necessary materials at hand. Your child will unconsciously learn from the care and attention that you put into these preparations.

+ ### Painting the Fables with Wet-on-Wet Water Colors

Wet-on-wet water painting is another medium with which to express the color, mood and forms of the fable images. With the crayons, the secondary colors arise from layering the colors and the forms arise from willfully controlling the grip on the crayon. With water paints the colors and forms occur in a freer and more spontaneous manner.

Although the forms arise from the colors, the brush strokes will capture the gesture of the land, plants, animals and figures, and further define the images.

Both mediums result in images that are impressionistic, with the illustrations merely suggesting the subject matter and conveying energy and mood, more than detail.

Perhaps you will choose to have your child do a series of watercolor paintings for the fables. If so, you can bind them together to make a Main Lesson book. Maybe the child could do the Main Lesson writing on separate pieces of paper which could then be glued onto the back of the finished paintings.

Children, familiar with the wet-on-wet technique from kindergarten and 1st grade, will want more control of their colors as they move into this next grade. The paper will be soaked in the same manner, and when put on the painting board should be dried to a slight moistness by spreading a clean terry cloth over it and patting lightly. The mixed colors will still be the primaries, with secondary colors available for certain effects. You can allow the color to settle in the jar and show the child how to use the sediment for areas of more intense color. You may wish to use slightly smaller brushes to more easily control the colors.

Remind the child not to overwork the painting. This is a transition time. Though very familiar with the freeness of his earlier painting, he may be inclined, at this point, to want to paint more literally. There are samples of water color illustrations for the fables starting on page 60.

♦ Modeling Figures from the Fables

One of the most effective ways of gaining a tactile, three dimensional sense of the animal characters is by modeling them.

It is important, when modeling, to remember that people and animals have one entire body, that our head and limbs are part of the whole. The child should be reminded to keep *intact* the piece of whatever medium he is given to model with. Head, limbs, and other parts that extend from the body, like tails, ears, horns, etc., should be drawn out of the whole of the substance, and *not* broken off, formed and then stuck back on. It is better to keep the form very simple than worry about shaping details that will interfere with the overall sense of the figure.

There are three popular modeling materials: Beeswax, Earth Clay and Play Dough.

Beeswax

One medium is modeling beeswax. The aromatic wax comes in little sheets in a variety of colors. The golden color most closely resembles the natural color of beeswax. Some children like to use multiple colors of wax. It is best to first create the main form from one color and then add a thin layer of the second color, than to build the whole from a number of parts. Refer to the Appendix on page 54 for sources for modeling beeswax.

The wax should be warmed in order to soften it enough to easily work with. This can be done in a number of ways. Generally, it is best to break a sheet of wax in half and form it into a lozenge shape that will fit into a child's cupped hands and be easy to work with. You can have the child hand warm the wax while listening to the story. The wax can also be softened by wrapping it in wax paper, tin foil or plastic wrap, and putting it in the sun, on a warm surface, or in warm, not hot, water. You want only to soften the wax, not melt it. There is a photograph of beeswax figures made by second graders on page 60.

Of course, you will want to tell the child how hard the bees must work to create this magical wax, as well as their sweet honey. This verse/ song can be repeated as the child takes his pieces of wax to model with.

> *The Bees*
> *Little bees work very hard,*
> *Making golden honey,*
> *Taking pollen from the flowers,*
> *When the days are sunny.*
> *Traditional*

This natural material has a lovely scent, and feels good on the hands. However, avoid it coming in contact with clothing as it will pick up the cloth fibers. It is best not to model directly on furniture, as the surface will cool the wax. Once the child feels that his/her form is finished and puts it down (perhaps on a special piece of wood or flat stone) it will harden and will not be able to be easily changed without softening it all over again.

After a period of time you may wish to recycle the wax figures. Whether the child sees you do this, or not, is up to you. (Some children may feel attached to their creations.) Simply soften the wax again and roll it out into a tablet shape, ready to be formed again another time.

Earth Clay

Many teachers feel that beeswax requires too much work, is too expensive, or for some other reason prefer earth clay. Earth clay, while almost always supple enough to model, can be very cooling to work with, as it is so damp. There are many children who do not care for the texture of the drying clay on their hands. If you are fortunate enough to have clay deposits in the earth near you, that the child can actually take from the ground, your child will most likely respond to it differently.

You may want to tell the child how clay has been used by mankind throughout time. Perhaps you will point out the different things in the home or classroom that were made of clay.

Since the clay figures will not be fired, they can easily be recycled, even after drying. The figures to be recycled should be broken into smaller pieces and put into a small bowl with some water sprinkled over them. (You might not want the children to see their work in pieces.) As the clay starts to soften add more water and kneed it. Eventually it will be at a malleable consistency.

Play Dough

Another modeling medium that children enjoy, but may be considered less orthodox is 'play dough.' 'Play dough' can easily be made from water, cornstarch and baking soda (see the recipe in the Appendix, page 54), but lacks the special connection to nature that bee's wax and clay have.

No matter which medium is used, by modeling the shapes of the animals, the child can learn so much with modeling in three dimensions. The child may even wish to use the figures they modeled to retell the fable with.

♦   The Fable Poem

In order to use poetry in your fable lesson you will need to either: write a poem, help your student to write one, or locate an existing poem about the fable or the characters in it.

By working with poetry, the child will experience a new way of hearing and using language, as well as learn yet another way to express him/herself. By reciting poetry the child has an opportunity to exercise proper enunciation (elocution) and develop his memory.

Out of numerous forms of poetry that you may work with, such as; rhymed, metered, haiku, free verse, and limericks, you will find in this case that a simple metered rhyme will work best. Meter, of course, means the rhythm in the line of poetry. You may wish to include alliteration and repetition in your verse. Certainly, if possible, you can make it humorous.

You might begin by writing down the key words about the animal or the events that you want your poem to be about. Then list several rhyming words after each of these. After you have exhausted your memory and imagination for sound-alike words, you can check for more words in a rhyming dictionary. But always first come up with your own list. You can even make a game out of it that will be sure to bring a lot of laughs.

For rhyming words to do with *bears*, the author came up with:

Bear: air, bare, care, dare, fair, fare, hair, lair, pair, rare, scare, share, spare,
         their, there, ware, wear, where
Brawn: gone, dawn, strong
Paw: claw, saw, straw, jaw
Burly: curly, early, swirly

Then, from the list of the most interesting rhyming words, create an opening line of your poem that ends with one of those words. Play with all the possibilities, and try for a second line. This following poem is the result of such an exercise. Though not great poetry, it shows how simple the process is.

The Bear

Where the hairy bear
Shares her lair
Is neither here nor there,
She bears a pair,
Who share her fare,
And bear her loving care

De Francesca

There are obvious rhymes at the end of each line of "*The Bear.*" Perhaps you will write your poem with every other line rhyming. Besides rhyming words, it is important to create a repeating beat or rhythm to your lines. Though "*The Bear*" has an uneven number of syllables in each line, it has a beat that helps with the recitation.

Weather or not you write the poem, or work with one that is well know, the child can still benefit so much by committing it to memory and reciting it, or even writing it out. Usually children are more able to quickly commit verses to memory than adults are. Repeat lines, then stanzas of the verse together with the child. Then speak the whole verse through a few times with the child. Lastly let the child try to recite it. When learning a verse it often helps to move to its rhythm. But, when reciting the poem, try to have the child stand and look at you as the words are spoken clearly.

Working with poetry can be a fun (and often amusing) activity to add to your lesson plans.

Special Activities for the Study of the Fables

By including a special activity to the lesson, beyond Main Lesson book writing and drawing, you add yet another facet to an already very rich program based on teaching a simple fable. When choosing the special activity, consider your child's needs. Is it time to include a simple natural science lesson to the curriculum? Would your child benefit from doing some theatre or puppetry? What about improvising or composing music around a fable?

If you have said "yes" to any of these points, then carefully plan how you might choose and incorporate a single special activity into your lesson plan.

These are just sparks, little ideas to stir your own creativity. As long as you find an activity that enlivens your child, that stretches his/her imagination, that awakens wonderment in some way, you are probably on the right track. Keep the activities as simple and uncomplicated as possible.

Keep in mind the intention of striving to teach what is *good, truthful* and *beautiful.* In other words, make sure that what is done by and for the child is wholesome, natural, and aesthetically pleasing. Avoid cartoon imagery and anthropomorphizing the characters. Animals in the wild do not wear clothes or have personal names, and so should not in the fables.

Do choose carefully from this abundant curriculum, to find the materials and activities that will best serve your child. A simple lesson plan, with elements that have been selected wisely, can be a richer experience than one that is overly complex. Above all, have fun!

♦ Puppet Shows of the Fables

Puppetry is a delightful craft and one not often considered as a teaching tool. Table, lap, hand, rod and shadow puppets are easy types of puppetry that can be used to effectively retell the fables.

Table Puppetry

Perhaps the simplest puppets to work with are table puppets. Any flat surface; a table, desks pushed together, or even the floor, will serve for the 'stage'. On this a scene can be set by arranging colored cloths over books or pieces of wood in order to create different surface levels for the puppets to move over. Additional use of rocks, branches, pine cones, foliage, and potted plants, as well as pieces of wood carved to resemble structures, will further define the scene.

Stuffed animals, knitted, stitched or felted (perhaps from a handwork class), or carved figures will serve well as the puppets. Try to keep the various characters in proper scale to each other. If there is a human character in the story, a well loved doll could be dressed to play the part.

For the performance, you will simply tell the story as you move the characters about the scene. Slow movements are preferable.

You may choose to have the scene covered with a light weight cloth, the 'curtain' that is lifted as you start the performance, and replaced again at the end.

Certainly the child will delight in performing the puppet show himself, afterwards, using the same puppets.

Lap Puppetry

Lap puppetry, in its simplicity, is an ideal way to perform the fable. The puppets would be much the same as the table puppets, though scaled smaller. For the stage and setting you need only to sit in an upright chair and drape colorful cloths over your chest and lap.

Because of limited space you will keep the scenery to a minimum. Puppets can be concealed behind the folds of cloth at your waist, until they are needed. You will control them just as you would the table puppets. A lap puppet play is usually "short and sweet."

Hand Puppetry

To offer a hand puppet performance of a fable may require quite a bit more preparation. Although a traditional puppet stage is not required, workable hand puppets will have to be created. These can be made by the teacher or student. Likewise, the teacher or the student can perform the puppet show.

Hand puppets generally consist of the character's head on some sort of 'glove-like' body. The heads can be stitched and stuffed, knitted, felted or formed of some other material, such as papier-mâché. The bodies need not be more than a tube shape, gathered at the neck, where the index finger fits through into the head. Since most of the fable characters are animals, their paws will rarely have to hold anything, so there will be little need to have the puppeteer's thumb and middle finger inside the animals' legs.

There are several simple ways of staging a hand puppet show. The easiest stage is achieved by spreading a cloth across the backs of 2 to 3 chairs and kneeling behind it. A waist high book case, or an upended table, will also make an effective stage. All that is really needed is a horizontal surface that conceals the forearms. It doesn't matter if the puppeteer's head shows as the audience's attention will be on the action of the puppets as the fable is being told.

You can improvise the setting with colorful cloths and /or cardboard pieces, creating hills, caves, bridges, fences, trees and the like.

Do avoid the slapstick kind of movements with the puppets that is so often seen in "Punch and Judy" plays. Subtlety is far more effective. So too, the voices you give to the puppets need not be disguised or silly.

Rod Puppetry

Though similar to hand puppetry, rod puppets are much simpler to produce. They can be easily made by cutting out a drawing or painting of the animal or character and taping a rod, stick, or bamboo skewer to the back to manipulate the figure with. You may want the figure illustrated on both sides so the character can face both directions.

Another form of rod puppets can be formed by inserting a knitting needle into the underside of a knitted, stuffed or felted animal and using that as the rod to animate it from below.

The puppets are then controlled from behind a panel or stage, much as hand puppets are.

Shadow Puppetry

Shadow puppetry is an unusual and effective medium for telling fables. Once you have made the screen with which to stage the show, you will find the creation and use of shadow puppets, for or by the students, is both easy and fun.

A semi-opaque screen is needed for the puppets to cast shadows on. The screen could measure anywhere from 9" X 18" to the size of a bed sheet. Smaller stages can be made by cutting an opening in the side of half of a large cardboard box and taping a piece of light weight drawing, or butcher paper over the opening. If you use a refrigerator box, it can then stand on the floor, if it's a smaller box, it can be placed on a desk or table. A larger screen can be made by stretching a white shower curtain, or a white sheet, on a rope (or wire) across a doorway or at the end of a room. For these larger screens you will need to define the area of the 'stage' or proscenium with an opaque cloth or a cardboard frame.

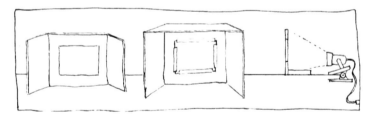

You will then need a source of light behind the screen with which to cast the shadow of the puppet onto the surface. Clamp-on LED lights (*little to no heat*) work well for smaller screens, where flood lights and (*much less safe, because of their intense heat*) halogen lights work for larger screens. There should be no light behind the puppeteer, just behind the puppets, and it is preferable that the audience be in a darkened area in order to add contrast to the shadows.

All of the images of a shadow puppet show are seen as silhouettes. The puppet figures are easily made from black construction paper. Draw the *side view* silhouette of the character, or set piece, with a white pencil on black paper and cut it out. Of course, these pieces will need to be proportional to each other, in order to create a workable scene. Any tears can easily be mended with clear tape. Tape the set pieces, trees, bridges, tables etc., in place on the screen.

As the shadow puppet scene is all in black and white, you may wish to add some color to liven it up. This can easily be done with colored cellophane (found in most craft stores, it comes on rolls) or special colored wax paper (the kind that is used for folded Christmas stars). Colored scenery, such as green rolling hills or blue ponds and rivers, can be quite effective. With a little imagination you can find ways to add color to the characters as well.

The puppets will require sticks to control their movement. Bamboo barbecue skewers are inexpensive and work well for this. To control the shadow puppet, tape the pointed end of the skewer to the back of the puppet with at least half the stick protruding from the bottom of the figure. (Black electrician's tape works well for this.) This is best done by cutting an 'L' shape of tape. Roll the bottom of the 'L' around the end of the stick. Attach the top part of the 'L' to the puppet.

For a more versatile and effective control mechanism, make a kind of hinge with the tape and hinge the end of the stick onto the center of the upper third of the puppet.

If you plan on having your puppet change directions, you can put the hinge at the top edge of the puppet. Practice by flipping the puppet over to make it easily face in both directions. This works particularly well if you want your puppet to fly. The object of these sticks, besides allowing you to easily hold the puppet, is to use them to press the puppet against the screen. By doing so, the shadow that is cast will have a sharp edge.

Do experiment with the many special effects you can achieve with this medium. You will find that the children will want to return again and again to shadow puppetry.

◆ The Fable as a Play

The improvised play is, by far, one of the easiest ways to have the child or children retell a fable. Depending on the number of children you are working with, and as the number of characters in the fables is usually quite limited, you may need to resort to creative ways to cast the play. You might have more than one child play a single roll at a time, or perhaps you can have different groups of children act out the story several different ways. Or, maybe one child will play all of the rolls. Remember, too, that children can become part of the scenery, such as trees, birds, or houses.

Some children are happy to be the director of the play, and, of course, there will have to be a narrator. What part, if any, will you, the teacher play?

As to staging technicalities, with an improvised play, the players are usually also the audience. Simply clear a place on the floor, decide who and what goes where, and begin.

Costumes and props are certainly optional. Sometimes a cloth over a chair, or a wooly cape on a player, is all that is needed. Usually there will be little need for a rehearsal. You might want to decide on a certain beginning and ending to your play, such as "Once upon a time" and "Stars and moon and sun, now our play is done." This will set it off as a proper play, instead of being just make believe play time.

If you wish to make the lesson into a creative writing exercise, why not have the child dictate and/or write out the script for the play? This can then be learned, a good memory exercise, and be performed for the delight of everyone.

✦ Music inspired by the Fable

Music is another form of expression that can be explored in relation to the fables. With a variety of instruments to play with (percussion, wind or string) a child can improvise or compose a piece around the fable, perhaps to the mood, the temperament, rhythm of the story, or sounds evoked by the animal characters. The music that results might be incorporated in a performance of a play or puppet show, or perhaps could be played with the fable poem, turning it into a song. Simple sound effects such as water pouring into a basin, a creaking door, etc. can
also be fun and very effective aural additions to a play.

✦ Natural Science Lesson in the Fables

It may seem strange to link a science lesson with a fable, but there are, in fact, several fables that suggest these unique links. Science, as a separate course, is not usually taught to seven, eight and nine year olds. But nature's scientific wonders, when
experienced in daily life, with familiar objects, can teach so much. What a magical thing it is to see the water level rise when one fills a bowl of water with beans, or to see how honey dissolves and disappears in a cup of hot tea. This is living science, mysterious and wondrous.

Some of the fables that contain these lessons include:

- *The Crow and the Pitcher*: water displacement
- *The Donkey and the Load of Salt:* dissolving salt, water absorption
- *The Dog and his Reflection:* reflection
- *The Oxen and the Wheels*: friction
- *The Wolf and his Shadow*: shadows
- *The Oak and the Reeds*: tensile strength

How might one present this *natural science lesson*? After telling the fable, you might want to briefly discuss the action that relates to the phenomena. "What about how that crow got the water to rise in the vase? Have you ever done something like that?" "What about the salt that donkey dissolved in the stream, have you ever seen something dissolve before? What happens when something dissolves?" "What about those sponges the donkey carried. Can you just guess how heavy they were when he came out of the water? Have you ever known something to get heavier when it's wet?" "Have you ever seen anything reflected in water before, like the dog did? Do you remember where?"

Then you should get some props ready to show the phenomenon. Maybe you will have a glass jar of water and some marbles ("Can you guess how many it will take before the jar overflows?"), a spoon full of sugar to dissolve in a glass cup of tea, or water in a dark bowl, to act like a mirror. Take a piece of chalk outdoors and draw around the child's shadow at different times of the day to see how the shadow's length changes. Show how easy it is to break one stick, and how difficult it is to break a bundle of them. There are so many ways that you can show these amazing facts of nature, and relate them to the fables you are teaching.

Do have fun with creating a holistic lesson plan around these marvelous fables. You will find that your imagination will be your best guide in bringing these diverse, multifaceted studies to your child. Enjoy!

Part 2   Expanded fables and renderings

Categorizing the Fables

Although most of Aesop's fables are the commonly known Animal Tales, many of the fables fall under other categories. There are:

- Animal Tales
    The Lion and the Mouse
    The Tortoise and the Hare
    The Town Mouse and the Country Mouse
    The Fox and the Grapes
    The Bear and the Bees
    Belling the Cat
    (and many, many more)

- Nature tales
    The Oak and the Reeds
    The North Wind and the Sun

- Tales with Humans
    The Shepherd and the Wolf
    The Travelers and the Bear
    The Goose that Laid Golden Eggs
    The Donkey and the Load of Salt
    Big and Little Fish
    The Boy who cried Wolf

- Tales with Natural Science Lessons
    The Too Fat Fox: volume of ice vs. water
    Big and Little Fish: scaling volume (use a sieve)
    The Crow and the Pitcher: water displacement
    The Donkey and the Load of Salt: dissolving salt, water absorption
    The Dog and his Reflection: reflection
    The Oxen and the Wheels: friction
    The Wolf and his Shadow: shadows
    The Oak and the Reeds: flexibility vs. rigidity

Three Sample Expanded Fables

What follows, are three expanded fables. Included in each section are pointers on how to extend the tales, as well as poems inspired by the fables and suggested special lesson activities related to the fable. Included is information regarding:

- Researching information for extending the tales
- Morals commonly attributed to fables
- Suggested expanded stories
- Illustrations for the fables; in crayon or watercolor
- Poems inspired by the fable or characters
- Special lesson activities

Aesop's fable of The Lion and the Mouse

The Fable

What follows is a traditional translation of an Aesop's fable. Note its simplicity, brevity and the obligatory moral at the end.

The Lion and the Mouse

Once when a Lion was asleep a little Mouse began running up and down upon him; this soon wakened the Lion, who placed his huge paw upon him, and opened his big jaws to swallow him. "Pardon, O King," cried the little Mouse: "forgive me this time, I shall never forget it: who knows what I may be able to do for you some day?" The Lion was so tickled at the idea of the Mouse being able to help him that he lifted up his paw and let him go. Some time after, the Lion was caught in a trap, and the hunters who desired to carry him alive to the King tied him to a tree while they went in search of a wagon to carry him. Just then the little Mouse happened to pass by, and seeing the sad plight in which the Lion was caught, went up to him and gnawed away the ropes that bound the King of the Beasts. "Was I not right?" said the little Mouse.

Moral: Little friends may prove great friends.

Research for Fable

Research from books and the internet can provide pertinent information to use when expanding and illustrating a fable. For the fable of *The Lion and the Mouse*, the author learned:

♦ Information about Lions

- Lions live in the plains, or savanna, which offer sufficient areas to hide
- Lions are large predators with tawny coats and manes that vary in color from black to blond
- Males are conspicuously large and showy
- Lions spend approximately twenty hours per day sleeping
- Lions are predatory carnivores who will resort to eating birds, rodents, fish and the like
- Lions have no natural predators, excepting humans
- Human poaching is a problem for lions

♦ Information about Mice

- Mice are small rodents
- They live in grasslands among other places
- Mice are low on the food chain
- Mice have the longest list of natural enemies of any known creature
- Mice must rely on their size, speed, and own ingenuity to survive
- Mice are unusually intelligent
- They will eat whatever they find
- Mice are unusually fast for their size

Morals Attributed to the Fable

The following morals are commonly attributed to this fable. Though it is interesting to see how others interpret the underlying meaning of a tale, it is important that you decide yourself what the essential message is, and extend the fable accordingly.

- No act of kindness, not matter how small, is ever wasted.
- Even the strong sometimes need the friendship of the weak.
- Little friends may prove great friends
- Even the weak and small may be of help to those much mightier than themselves.

The Expanded Story

The following version of Aesop's *The Lion and the Mouse* is an example of how a fable might be expanded to contain information about the animal characters and make the tale a longer and more engaging. Again, since the moral is not told at the end of the story, the story should develop in such a manner that the listener will be able to easily identify it by him or herself.

The Lion and the Mouse

The sun glared down on the vast open grasslands. Waves of shimmering heat hung over the day. There was not a sound, nothing stirred, no flies buzzed, nor grasshopper sawed. All were too hot.

There, under a straggly old tree that was all but bare of leaves, lay a great lion. Though massive and majestic, known by all as the King of the Beasts, he could hardly be seen as he lay there so still, his tawny coat the color of the sun dried grasses. He slept. Maybe he dreamt he was a giant, ruling over his Pride, his royal lion family. Maybe he dreamt that he was dashing swiftly across the plains, quickly gaining on a hoofed animal. Maybe he dreamt that he had just won a battle with another powerful lion. The king slept on. Woe to anyone who would disturb him.

The sun moved slowly and lazily across the sky. And still, all was quiet.

But wait, what was that? What was that that scurried across the dirt path, kicking up the tiniest cloud of dust? A mouse. A little thing, all sandy grey with shiny bright eyes. Quick, there it goes again, from one clump of grass to another, zigzagging across the path, looking for grains, for something to eat in that hot, parched place.

Such a tiny thing was the mouse, it's no wonder he didn't even notice the great lion lying there. Seeing yet another clump of grass, he stretched, reaching up and bent down a tall stalk, hoping to find some seeds. The blade's spiky tip brushed across the lion's great nose.

At once a large amber colored eye blinked open. The same instant a massive paw with blade like claws crashed down on the mouse's tail, the claws just missing him.

"Who dares, disturb my sleep?" roared the lion.

The little mouse was at once speechless, unable to move because of the great paw trapping his delicate tail.

"So?" said the lion irately. "Speak!"

"Oh, Your Majesty," squeaked the mouse as he looked up, so surprised to see the lion. "It must have been me. I am so very sorry. You are so grand, and I am so small. Oh, please do not hurt me!"

"And why should I not? I would like to know?" mussed the lion, as he slowly lifted his great paw.

The mouse thought quickly. "Why, your Majesty, who knows, perhaps I could return the favor for you someday."

"What is that? You help me? Me, the King of Beasts? Ha, ha! Ha, ha! You are making me laugh. It is too, too hot to laugh. Be off with you. Ha!! What an idea, a tiny weak mouse help the great King!"

The little mouse wasted no time and quickly scurried away. The great lion soon tired of the joke and fell sound asleep. The sun continued to inch its way towards the horizon. It was then that it happened.

Suddenly, seemingly out of nowhere, a great heavy net of thick rope was thrown over the lion. Though the lion awoke immediately from his sleep, he was so confused that he did not move to run before several men had hammered stout spikes into the ground to hold the net fast. Oh, but the lion did roar!

He roared and roared. He bellowed and growled. The men went away. He roared some more. The great, mighty King was a prisoner, he was trapped. One might think that other lions would come to his aid, for his roars were heard for miles. But all were too fearful, so angry did he seem.

Then someone did come. It was the wee little mouse. With caution, but with purpose the mouse crept along the ground. He ignored the thrashing, howling of the lion and jumped up onto a spike and crawled onto one of the knots of rope. And he began to do what mice can do so well, he nibbled. He nibbled and nibbled and nibbled at those thick ropes that held the King so tightly.

Though his heart was small, his caring was great. The lion had spared his life and now was in need. His size did not matter. When he saw the mouse, the lion stopped roaring, stopped thrashing. In a short time the mouse had completed his task, the rope was chewed through and the lion was at last, freed.

The lion could have dashed off without any thanks. But with true greatness comes humbleness. The lion, the King of Beasts, was well aware of what the mouse had done. There, in the ruddy light of the setting sun, the lion paused, looked down at the little mouse. "Thank you," he said, and then turned and leapt away.

"Stars and moon and sun, now my story's done."

Illustrations

The purpose behind guiding a child to copy a picture that you draw is to teach him a *vocabulary of expression*. With practice, the child learns to draw animals, learns to draw people, learns to draw landscapes, etc. Very soon then the child will able to use these abilities to assemble their own images using the learned vocabulary.

◆   Illustrating the Fable with Block Crayons

On page 59 is a simple block crayon drawing of a lion and a mouse. Below it you will find the artwork of a second grader who has copied the techniques, having been guided through the process. One can easily see how similar the child's picture is to the teacher's, but also how delightful the differences are.

As a teacher, you will first draw the image yourself, before you draw it again, when guiding the student. The directions to creating the image follow:

1. Commence by drawing a yellow (large side) band across, and a couple inches above, the bottom of the page. This is the ground line. It establishes the foundation for the image, and indicates the earth for the lion to lie on.
2. Imagine that you are petting a cat, which the lion actually is, and feel the gesture your hand makes along the head and spine of the lion. Now, with your finger only, trace that line on your paper where you want your lion's back to be. When you can really imagine it there, draw it as a yellow (medium side) band, not line, of color. Use yellow in case you need to make adjustments.
3. With yellow (medium side) create a round cloud of color that will be the lion's head, and mane. Do not outline, but draw the color from the center out to the periphery. Similarly, fill in the mass of the lion's body with yellow.
4. Draw, with yellow (medium side) the lion's front legs curving down towards the bottom of the page.
5. At the rump part of the lion, first with yellow, then with red (medium side) lightly draw a large 'S' shape to indicate the lion's haunch and leg, drawing the bottom of the 'S' down towards the bottom of the page. Fill in the leg, adjusting its thickness and color.
6. Draw the tail, curving around the back of the lion. Add a tuft to the end of it.
7. Look at the general proportions of the yellow lion and make any needed adjustments.
8. *Lightly* draw over your lion with red (medium side) to make it a nice orange color.
9. With red (medium) draw two curved areas at the top of the face for the ears.
10. With red and yellow (medium) draw a circle of radiating lines around the head (face) of the lion. This will be the mane. Remember, to always start with a light touch, as you can make your images darker later, but not lighter.
11. Very lightly with red, draw a mark for the lion's nose. Then draw, again very lightly, two curved lines to indicate the lion's facial features. This is optional.
12. Draw the mouse as a small oval shape with blue (small side), between the lion's forepaws. Add a thin line for its tail and suggest the tiny ears.

13. With the large side of both red and yellow crayons, draw bands curving around, and off the edge of, the border of the paper. This encircles the animals with a soft, embracing frame of colored atmosphere.
14. Go over the entire picture with yellow (avoiding the mouse), to give the image a fiery glow.

Take your time when doing your drawings and urge your child to do the same. With care and practice you will be able to draw these and other images with ease.

* Illustrating the Fable with Water Colors

Painting these images with wet-on-wet water paints can be very satisfying. Follow the directions given above (for coloring with block crayons) to paint the image. The steps are essentially the same. You may wish to experiment with the paint brush to find ways to vary the width of your brush strokes. Though these images can be created with just the primary colors, you may want to introduce some gold color, or orange, to enhance the lion, perhaps in his mane and tail. There is a sample painting of this illustration on page 60.

* Modeling the Fable Characters with Beeswax

The modeling beeswax, when adequately warmed, should be easy to form with. To guide the child how to make a lion make the following suggestions. See some beeswax lions created by second graders on page 60.

1. Start by forming the wax into an egg shape.
2. Draw the head shape out a bit, and press around the neck area.
3. Draw a thin, tufted tail out of the back of the shape.
4. Draw and form the forelegs out of the wax of the body. Do not attach separate pieces.
5. Then, with only a few adjustments, the form is done.

If desired, a small mouse can be made, as well.

1. With blue wax (any color is fine) again start with an egg shape.
2. Point the end, for the nose, and pinch little ears at the top.
3. To finish it off, draw a tail out from the other end and work it until it is long and thin.

You may wish to display the figures on a piece of bark or arrange them on your nature table.

The Fable Poem

There are numerous poems and nursery rhymes about mice that you could use with this lesson. Or, perhaps you will want to write your own. The author has attempted, in the poem below, to retain some of the same language and imagery that is in the story.

The Lion and the Mouse

Beneath the brassy sun, in grasses high,
A fierce, but lazy, lion did lie.

Then crept by a mouse, on tiny feet,
Who awoke the lion, who there did sleep.

Said the lion to the one so small,
"How dare you rouse the King of All?

I could eat you in one bite,
Then go back to sleep 'till night."

"Your majesty, please, don't hurt me
Please, let me go, please, set me free.

Perhaps some time, I could help you.
You might be surprised what I can do."

"You help me? Ha! That I would see.
Go, little one, be off. You are free."

Off went the mouse, and the great lion slept,
And much later, towards him, two hunters crept.

Way before the red sun set,
That the lion was bound in a great, rope net.

While the hunters went off for a helping hand,
The lion's loud roar was heard over the land.

He gnashed and bellowed, he growled and he tore,
'Till that meek little mouse crept before him once more.

Quickly the mouse jumped up on the net,
While he nibbled and nibbled, the lion did fret.

Soon with his hard work, he had set the King free,
The King, to be sure, was as glad as could be.

The two of them now call each other a friend,
And that is how this story does end.

De Francesca

Special Activities

Besides retelling the story as a creative writing exercise, or writing his own poem about one of the characters, there are numerous other ways that the child may be inspired by this fable. This story can easily be acted out with two, to even a dozen, players. Beyond the obvious two animals, additional players could take other parts: the animals that show deference to the King, the hunters, the tree, and even the stakes holding the net down. If there are still players who want a role, perhaps the lion's dreams could be acted out. And don't forget the narrator.

It would be easy enough to tell the story as a table puppet show. Stuffed or felted animals would serve well, or perhaps the main characters could be knitted as a handwork project. You might even want to go outside in the garden and act out the story with objects found in nature.

The story could be just as effectively performed as a rod or shadow puppet show.

Don't forget that the forms of the lion and the mouse can be formed from a number of different modeling mediums, and that those figures might be used the next lesson to retell the fable.

One would have to be pretty imaginative to come up with a natural science lesson related to this fable. Perhaps you could make an example of the effects of friction by wearing through a piece of rope with a small, sharp stone. Thus the child could experience the hard work and persistence required for the little mouse to succeed in nibbling through the ties that held the lion.

Be creative and above all, have fun!

Aesop's fable of The Bear and the Bees

The Fable

What follows is a traditional translation of another Aesop's fable. Note its simplicity, brevity and the obligatory moral at the fable's end.

The Bear and the Bees

A bear came across a log where a swarm of bees had nested to make their honey. As he snooped around, a single little bee flew out of the log to protect the swarm. Knowing that the bear would eat all the honey, the little bee stung him sharply on the nose and flew back into the log.

This flew the bear into an angry rage. He swatted at the log with his big claws, determined to destroy the nest of bees inside. This only alerted the bees and quick as a wink, the entire swarm of bees flew out of the log and began to sting the bear from head to heel. The bear saved himself by running to and diving into the nearest pond.

Moral: It is better to bear a single injury in silence than to bring about a thousand by reacting in anger.

Research

Research from books and the internet can provide pertinent information to use when expanding and illustrating a fable. For the fable of *The Bear and the Bees*, the author learned:

- Information about Bears

  - Bears live mostly in forested areas
  - Bears, like people, have different colored hair (fur)
  - Bears are omnivores; they eat mostly insects, plants, grasses, leaves, flowers, mushrooms, berries and other fruit and nuts
  - Bears eat honey, but like the bees and larvae best, honey is an extra treat
  - Bear's sense of smell is better than that of most animals, can smell food a mile or more away
  - Bear's lips are sensitive; they use their lips to touch, like humans do with fingers
  - Bears stand up a lot, to see better
  - Bears can run for a short distance, as fast as 35 mph.
  - Bears are good swimmers
  - Bears are usually quiet, but make sounds: huffing, woofing, chomping, moaning, grunting and snorting

♦ Information about Bees

- The bee's weapon is a barbed stinger which can be used once before it kills the bee
- Male bees cannot sting
- When the hive is threatened, bees swarm out, attack with their stingers to drive the enemy away
- Bees work together in a structured social order of one queen, workers and drones
- Workers maintain and operate the hive, tend the queen and drones, clean, regulate temperature, and defend the hive
- Older workers forage outside to gather nectar, pollen, water and resins for hive construction
- Workers have pollen basket on each hind leg
- Bees eat flower nectar and pollen

♦ Information about the hive and honey

- A honeycomb is made of flat vertical panels of six-sided beeswax cells
- Cells hold young bees and store honey
- Honey is a thick liquid produced from the nectar of flowers
- Bees refine and concentrate nectar to make the honey as food for winter

Morals for the Fable

The following morals are commonly attributed to this fable. Though it is interesting to see how others interpret the underlying meaning of a tale, it is important that you decide yourself what the essential message is, and extend the fable accordingly.

- Anger, a negative trait and bad habit, often brings injury and grief to others, though sometimes only to the person who's lost control.
- Forgiveness and tolerance are two qualities to help keep one's anger in check.
- It's wiser to bridle one's anger over a trifling injury than to risk a thousand more. Getting mad over little things can make it worse.
- It is wiser to bear a single injury in silence than to provoke a thousand by flying into a rage.

Expanded Story

The following version of Aesop's *The Bear and the Bees* is an example of how a fable might be expanded to contain information about the animal characters and make the tale a longer and more engaging. Again, since the moral is not told at the end of the story, the story should develop in such a manner that the listener will be able to easily identify it by him or herself.

The Bear and the Bees

Deep in the forest there is a clearing. There the sun shines into a bright little valley where a sparkling stream gurgles. The place is alive with tender green grasses and splashes of bright colored flowers. There are big boulders, some fallen trees and other trees that grow strong and upright. There, between two great branches that reach out from an old gnarled trunk is a great buzzing of activity.

That is the royal palace of the bees. The revered Queen is deep inside the waxy halls of the hive, tended to day and night by her ladies in waiting, the busy worker bees. They feed her and clean her, and keep her at just the right temperature.

The Queen is busy laying eggs - Many eggs that will grow to be new workers. These workers will venture out into the colorful world of flowers to bring back nectar to make into honey, and pollen for food, and the stuff to make waxen rooms, or cells, for the babies to grow in and for the food and honey to be stored in. Some of the Queen's eggs will grow to be drones, lazy princes who will have little to do in their short lives. A very few of the eggs will grow to be princesses and eventually queens themselves.

Now let us look out in the bright world again, away from the dark, honey scented palace hive that lies deep within the old tree trunk. In the sunlight the workers lazily swarm about, coming and going.

Those bees who are returning have big 'baskets' on their hind legs, all bright gold from the pollen that they gathered from many flowers. The bees who are just leaving have nothing to hold them down, for they have literally thousands of blossoms to visit to make the tiniest bit of honey for the queen. Some of the workers are guards. They hover about the tree, always on the lookout for a thief who will break in and steal the gold, or worse yet, harm the precious Queen.

Some distance away, lumbering through the forest is altogether another kind of creature, the great shaggy bear. Bear is celebrating this time of plenty, for it is the glorious summer. Such wonderful smells invite him here and there.

There is always something yummy to eat. What is that smell that calls to him there under the fallen log? Oh, yes, tender mushrooms. What is that sweet smell coming from? What are those glowing colors in that small patch of sunlight? Ah, it's a berry bush.

Carefully he approaches it, his tender nose sniffing out the berries, while his massive clawed paw pulls back the prickly branches so he can access the fruit.
Uh, oh, what was that sound? Something dropped out of the tree? Ah ha, a silly squirrel dropped some acorns. Yummy crunch and the nuts are soon gone.

The bumbling bear snuffled and munched his way through the woods. Soon fall would come. By then the bear should have grown nice and fat so he could sleep all the way through the winter.

Down by the stream the bear's big claws swoop into the water, flicking out a dancing, shining fish. What a garden of plenty is this forest. He stops, he pauses and listens. Off in the distance an eagle keens. And then silence.

But is it silence? By now the bear is in the sunny valley, not far from a particular old tree. He listens again, and hears a soft buzz. "What is that?" he wonders. He stands up on his hind legs to see and hear better. Again, he hears the buzz, but it is now stronger, because he is now facing towards it. And he remembers, remembers a time long ago when his mother was near such a buzzing, and came to him all covered with sticky sweetness.

He made his way over to the tree and looked up. The cloud of amber colored bees became more animated. But closer now, the smell of the honey treasure was stronger. Again the bear stood, leaned against the tree and thrust his nose right to the sweet smelling crack in the bark.

There, right by the entrance, fresh on duty, flew a young worker bee. She knew what her responsibility was.

She flew right to the great snuffling nose that was intruding the palace and, sacrificing herself, thrust her little stinger into its flesh.

The bear snorted and grunted in pain. Oh, how that hurt. Blinding anger swelled up in him. He was furious! No little insect would sting him on the nose and keep him from the sweet treasure!

The bear faced the tree, and with a mighty, angry swat, he hit at the bark doorway with his great clawed paw. All this accomplished though was to summon the rest of the guards. At once, all of the queen's workers attacked!

In no time the bear's head was caught in a dark, stinging cloud of pain. His tender nose was like one big wound. He turned and ran. He ran faster than you might have thought him capable, being so fat. He ran to the stream and buried his painful nose in the cool mud at the stream's edge, trying to find some relief from the agonizing stings. But the bees were in hot pursuit, so he quickly dove into the cold water, and swam away as fast as he could.

"Stars and moon and sun, now my story's done."

Illustrations

As stated before, the purpose behind guiding a child to copy the picture you draw is to teach them a *vocabulary of expression*. With practice, the child learns to draw animals, learns to draw people, learns to draw landscapes, etc. Very soon then the child will able to use these abilities to assemble their own images using the learned vocabulary.

◆   Illustrating the Fable with Block Crayons

On page 61 is a simple block crayon drawing of the bear fleeing the angry bees. You, the teacher, should first practice drawing the image yourself, before you draw it again while guiding the student. The directions to creating the image follow:

1. Commence by drawing a yellow (large side) band across and a 2-3 inches above the bottom of the page. This is the ground line. It establishes the foundation for the image, the ground across which the bear will be running.

2. The bear's back is quite distinctive, with a hump of muscle at the shoulder. The silhouette of the back is a broad undulating line. Practice the gesture of the bear's spine in the air with your hand. Then, with finger only, draw that shape on the page. It helps to look at a sample picture of a bear. When you can really imagine it on the page, draw it as a yellow (medium side) band of color. Use yellow in case you need to make adjustments.

3. With yellow (medium side) fill in the mass of the bear's body. Do not outline, but draw the color from the center out. Define the shape of the head as best as possible. Show the roundness of the bear's rump. Extend the feet in both directions to indicate flight.

4. With red (medium side) draw over the form of the bear, accentuating shaded areas, as suggested in the sample. Remember, to always start with a light touch, as you can make your images darker later, but not lighter.

5. Lightly draw in ears, nose, and tail. If you wish to give your bear an eye, merely suggest it with a slightly darker color.

6. If you wish to make the bear a browner color, add a light touch of blue (medium side) over the orange color of the fur.

7. Draw in the stream with blue (medium side) bands of color. Use soft, wavy, flowing strokes to show the movement of the water.

8. Go over the rest of the drawing with yellow (avoiding the stream), even going over the bear to warm the color of his fur.

9. With blue (medium side) lightly create a green for the grass under and around the bear's feet.

10. With red (medium side) 'plant' an imaginary seed on the ground behind the bear. Lightly, with a graceful stroke 'grow' the trunk of the tree upwards and then branch it outwards. Go over this with yellow and a touch of blue if you wish. Add clouds of yellow, and then blue, to the branches to create the leaves (if you wish for your tree to have leaves). You may wish to indicate the place on the tree where the bee's hive is, perhaps with a touch of gold crayon where the branches join.

11. With the corner of the red crayon, make light dots for the bees, swarming them around the bear's head and across its back, ending back at the tree.

12. Go over the picture with yellow, pressing hard in places, to give the image a sunny glow. If you go over the red dots of the bees, *towards* the direction of their hive, with the strokes of yellow, it will create the appearance of motion, as if the bees were flying away from the hive.

Take your time when doing your drawings and urge your child to do the same. With care and practice you will be able to draw these and other images with ease.

◆ Illustrating the Fable with Water Colors

Painting these images with the wet-on-wet painting technique can be very satisfying. Follow the directions given above (for coloring with block crayons) to paint the image. The steps are essentially the same. Though these images can be created with just the primary colors, you may wish to introduce some gold color to the tree to indicate the honey. After all is painted but the bees, wait until the painting dries a bit. Then you can paint the bees in with the tiniest dots of red or gold with the corner of your brush. There is a sample painting of this illustration on page 61.

◆ Modeling the Fable Characters with Beeswax

The wax, when adequately warmed, should be easy to model with. Guide the child how to make a bear that is simply standing still.

1. Start by forming the wax into an egg shape.

2. Draw the head out, and press around the neck area.

3. Make the nose slightly pointed. Pinch out tiny ears.

4. Draw out the wax for the legs. Keep them short and thick.

5. Work on the shoulder and rump to keep them high and rounded.

6. Then, with only a few adjustments the form is done.

You might like to display the bear, or bears, on a piece of bark, or put them on your nature table.

The Fable Poem

In place of writing one poem to tell the story of the whole fable, one might write short poems about the characters.

The Bear

Where the hairy bear
Shares her lair
Is neither here nor there,
She bears a pair,
Who share her fare,
And bear her loving care.
De Francesca

The Bees

Little bees work very hard,
Making golden honey,
Taking pollen from the flowers
When the days are sunny.
Traditional

Special Activities

Besides retelling the story as a creative writing exercise, or writing a poem about the characters, or the fable, there are several other ways that the child may be inspired by working with this fable.

Though it might not be as easy to act this story out as a play, it could be easy enough to tell the story as a table puppet show. A stuffed, knitted or felted bear could be created as a handwork project, as could some tiny bees. See instructions in the Appendix (page 55) for how to make a little bee puppet that hangs on a thread. Perhaps, for the play, a number of these could be made and hung from a small branch. A potted plant or a small tree branch could serve as the tree with the hive. You might even want to go outside in the garden and act out the story with things from nature.

The story could be just as effectively performed as a shadow puppet show. The swarm of bees could be tiny shapes drawn or stuck onto a piece of clear cellophane that is moved across the screen. Perhaps you could come up with another way of representing the bees.

Don't forget that the forms of the bear and the tiny bees can be modeled out of a number of different modeling mediums, and that those figures might be used the next lesson to retell the fable.

For the natural science lesson around this fable, you could find different methods of creating bee sounds, perhaps by blowing on wax paper over a comb, like a kazoo, or plucking a tightly stretched rubber band. Or, maybe you could find some honey with the honeycomb still in it. After examining the delicate wax cells you could have a special treat of toast and honey. What other ideas can you think of?

What ever you choose do to will add fresh facets to your fable lesson. Have fun!

Aesop's fable of The Crow and the Pitcher

The Fable

What follows is a traditional translation of yet another Aesop's fable. Note its simplicity, brevity and the obligatory moral at the end.

The Crow and the Pitcher

A crow perishing with thirst saw a pitcher, and hoping to find water, flew to it with delight. When he reached it, he discovered to his grief that it contained so little water that he could not possibly get at it. He tried everything he could think of to reach the water, but all his efforts were in vain.

At last he collected as many stones as he could carry and dropped them one by one with his beak into the pitcher, until he brought the water within his reach and thus saved his life.

Moral: Necessity is the mother of invention.

Research for the Fable

Research from books and the internet can provide pertinent information to use when expanding and illustrating a fable. For the fable of *The Crow and the Pitcher*, the author learned:

◆ Information about Crows

- ◆ Crows are generally black with black beaks and legs
- ◆ Crows can be found just about anywhere: mountains, woodlands, plains, fields, and urban areas
- ◆ Crows will eat anything edible and many things which aren't
- ◆ Crows eat many pests which are harmful to crops
- ◆ Crows are highly intelligent birds who have been known to make and use tools
- ◆ Any scarecrow which remains in the same place for several days quickly becomes a perch rather than a warning sign to crows

Morals for the Fable

The following morals are commonly attributed to this fable. Though it is interesting to see how others interpret the underlying meaning of a tale, it is important that you decide yourself what the essential message is, and extend the fable accordingly.

- Thoughtfulness is superior to brute strength.
- Persistence is the way to success.
- Necessity is the mother of invention.
- Little by little does the trick.

The Expanded Story

The following version of Aesop's *The Crow and the Pitcher* is an example of how a fable might be expanded to contain information about the animal characters and make the tale a longer and more engaging. Again, since the moral is not told at the end of the story, the story should develop in such a manner that the listener will be able to easily identify it by himself.

The Crow and the Pitcher

High above the world flew the shiny black crow. Below, the land was a quilt of fields, all different shades of gold. It was late summer and many of the crops were being harvested.

"Caw, caw!" called the bird as it curved down in a great spiral through the thick hot air. "Caw!" it cried as it landed on its favorite roost.

There, out in the middle of the field a farmer had so kindly built a padded perch for him, so that he, the crow, might survey what goes on from in all corners of the countryside. Curious thing, that perch, for it looked much like the farmer himself, standing there with his hay stuffed arms outstretched in welcome.

Today the crow was thirsty. He had successfully gleaned some corn from the field, and had found some good grubs under a stone, but the river was a long flight away, and the hot air was too dry.

"Certainly the field workers have some water," he thought to himself as he lifted off into the shimmering, chaff-filled air. Even the flies and bees were lazy in the heat, buzzing sleepily. In the distance a cicada shrilled out its loud protest to the sun.

The crow circled over the harvesters as they crouched to their work. He saw that they had already moved across the field, and were some distance from where they had had lunch.

48

"Caw!" he called out, "surely they will have left something for me." And in one lazy waft of his wings he swooped down to their lunching place by an old tree at the edge of the field. "Caw!" he squawked in delight. Yes, there were the scattered remains of their lunch; the rough end of a brown loaf, a dry curled rind of cheese, and a pitcher.

Normally, the crow would have made short order of the food scattered there, but the water that was surely in the pitcher, was for him, so thirsty he was.

Hop, hop, hop, he leapt right up to it, and thrust his beak inside ready to quench his thirst. But, what is this? His beak could not reach the water! He pulled back, cocked his head and looked down into the darkness of the jug. Yes, there was water there, but how was he to get to it?

The crow looked around. Scattered about the area were some stones. "Yes," said the crow to himself. "These will do the trick." He took a stone into his strong beak and dropped it into the pitcher. What a lovely sound was the watery splash he heard there. Another and another stone followed. Splash plunk, splash plunk, splash plunk!

He stopped and cocked his head again to look down, and to his delight could see a little circle of the sky reflected in the water. He dropped in a couple more stones. Then, standing with his claws firmly apart, he thrust his beak once again into the pitcher and this time drank. He drank and drank until his thirst washed away. As if he were flying through a soft rain, he drank his fill. He then hopped over and snatched that piece of cheese and flew to his favorite roost to enjoy his wonderful world.

"Stars and moon and sun, now my story's done."

Illustrations

As stated before, the purpose behind guiding a child to copy the picture you draw is to teach him a *vocabulary of expression*. With practice, the child learns to draw animals, learns to draw people, learns to draw landscapes, etc. Very soon then the child will able to use these abilities to assemble their own images using the learned vocabulary.

◆ Illustrating the Fable with Block Crayons

On page 62 is a block crayon drawing of the crow dropping stones into the pitcher. You, as the teacher, should first practice drawing this image yourself, before you draw it again while guiding the student. The directions to creating the image follow:

1. Commence by drawing a yellow (large side) band across, and a couple inches above, the bottom of the page. This is the ground line. It establishes the foundation for the image, the ground across which the crow and the pitcher will be standing.

2. The crow's back gives it a quite distinctive shape, with a slight hump at the shoulder. Practice drawing the gesture of the crow's silhouette in the air with your finger.

3. Then, with finger only, draw that shape on the page. It helps if you look at a sample picture.

4. When you can really imagine it there, draw it as a *very pale* blue (medium side) band of color.

5. Then, fill in the mass of the crow's body. Do not outline it, but draw the color from the center out. Remember, to always start with a light touch, as you can make your images darker later, but not lighter.

6. Go back over the body of the bird to make it darker. Draw the wings, tail, beak and legs last. You might want to add touches of red to the blue to darken the color of the crow's body.

7. With yellow (medium side) draw in the shape of the pitcher very lightly. Try to place it under the crow's head. It is okay if the bottom of the pitcher comes lower than the crow's feet as you could draw a rock under the crow's feet. When you are happy with the pitcher, draw over it with red, to make an orange color.

8. Color in the ground with yellow (large side) and then over it with blue or red, depending on that color you want it to be.

9. If you wish to draw a tree in the background, do so now. Remember to "plant" an imaginary seed on the ground behind the bear. Lightly, with a graceful stroke "grow" the trunk of the tree upwards and branch it outwards.

10. Go over the rest of the drawing with yellow, avoiding the crow. This will warm the picture.

11. With either red or blue (large side) draw off the edge of the paper all across the bottom edge of the paper and up the sides in graceful bands to frame in the image with color.

Take your time when doing your drawings and urge your child to do the same. With care and practice you will be able to draw these and other images with ease.

♦   Illustrating the Fable with Water Colors

Painting these images with wet-on-wet water paints can be very satisfying. Follow the directions given above (for coloring with block crayons) to paint the image. The steps are essentially the same. You may wish to experiment with the paint brush to find ways to vary the width of your brush strokes. There is a sample painting of this illustration on page 62.

The Fable Poem

With this poem an attempt has been made to retain the language and mood of the extended fable. You will find that the student will be able to learn it very quickly, after only a few repetitions.

The Crow and the Pitcher

Round great circles in the sky
The thirsty crow one summer did fly.
Down he spiraled to the field
To see what harvest it would yield.
He alighted on a scarecrow bold
And looked across the field of gold.
Toiling beneath the brassy sun,
Were workers who thought
they'd never be done.

Far beneath a tree there lay,
The remains of their meal,
From that day.
The crow with intent to slack his thirst
Flew over to their pitcher first.
The water level was too low,
To his dismay.
Was he ever to drink
On this hot day?
Then many stones into the jug he tipped,
Till the water rose and the crow sipped.
He drank and drank the pitcher dry
Then back to his scarecrow he did fly.

De Francesca

Special Activities

Besides retelling the story as a creative writing exercise, or writing his own poem, there are numerous other ways that the child may be inspired by working with this fable.

Since this is not really an action story, you might not choose to bother with performing it as a play. However, it could make a rather fun and effective shadow puppet show. Why not come up with fun sound effects to accompany it?

Or, you might have the student shape the form of the crow and a pitcher out of a modeling medium. These might then be used the next lesson to retell the fable.

This fable does contain an interesting natural science lesson: measuring water volume and displacement. Of course you would not teach it as such, but instead you might have a glass vase half full of water and show how your fingers, with tips together, cannot fit to the bottom of the vase to get to the water, much as the crow's beak could not. Then you might have some colorful marbles, or let the child go into the yard to retrieve a number of pebbles, and then put the pebbles, one by one into the vase, all the time watching the water level rise. You could even have the child guess how many more pebbles would be needed before the water reached the rim of the vase.

Ask if the child has seen something make the water level rise before. Perhaps when they take a bath? When a lot of potatoes were put in a basin of water to wash? This can be a fun time for discussion. This lesson, like the other suggested science lessons, helps to awaken the child to the world around him, and see the magic in the simplest phenomena.

In Summary

The above three, expanded fables, and suggestions for the different facets of study related to them, are meant to be samples to inspire you to extend your own fables and create enjoyable, creative, holistic lessons for your children.

Please do not try to do *all of the activities* that are suggested here with *each* fable, but use them as inspiration. Draw from these ideas to tailor them to your own specific needs.

You will find, no matter what subject you are teaching, that there are basic elements to creating a truly holistic lesson plan for the whole child. These include:

- Teaching to the *head, heart and hand*
- Creating an organic rhythm in the lesson
- Conveying a sense of *reverence* for the material
- Including some form of *ritual* in the lesson
- *Reviewing* work from the previous lesson
- Introducing at least *one new thing* with each lesson
- *Rendering* the material in an artistic medium

Discover ways to apply these elements to the lessons you teach and you will see how alive they become, making teaching and learning a joy. Do be creative and above all, have fun!

Teach Wonderment!

Appendix

Categorization of 25 Aesop's Fables (see page 17)

Fable	Animal	Human	Moral Message	Value	Warning Against	Dramatic Story	Natural Science Lesson
The Ass & the Load of Salt	√	√	Same measures will not suit all circumstances	forbearance	trickery	√	solution, weight of water
The Bear & the Bees	√		Best bear a single injury, than cause a thousand through anger	tolerance	rage	√	
The Boy who cried Wolf	√	√	Liars are never believed even when speaking the truth	honesty	deceit	√	
The Bundle of Sticks		√	In unity is strength	unity		√	tensile strength
The Crow & the Pitcher	√		Necessity is mother of invention	intelligence		√	water displacement
The Deer & his Antlers	√	√	We adore the ornamental & despise the useful	acceptance	vanity	√	
The Dog & his Reflection	√		It is very foolish to be greedy		greed		reflection
The Farmer & his Sons		√	Industry is itself a treasure	industry		√	soil cultivation
The Field Mouse & the House Mouse	√		Secure poverty is better than uncertain riches	tolerance, adaptability	pride	√	
The Fox & the Crow	√		The flatterer lives at the expense of those who will listen to him	acceptance	pride	√	gravity
The Fox & the Grapes	√	√	Don't naysay what is out of reach	acceptance	self deception	√	
The Fox & the Stork	√		Treat others as you would be treated	kindness	revenge	√	
The Goose & the Golden Egg	√	√	Those who have plenty want more & so loose what they have	patience	greed	√	reproduction
The Grasshopper & the Ant	√		To work today is to eat tomorrow	diligence	laziness	√	
The Hare & the Tortoise	√		Slow & ready wins the race	perseverance	laziness	√	
The Heron	√		Don't be too picky or you will end up with nothing	acceptance	choosiness		
The Lion & the Mouse	√	√	Even the small can be powerful	kindness		√	friction
The Milkmaid & her Pail		√	Don't count your chickens before they hatch	patience	pride, greed	√	balance
The North Wind & then Sun		√	Gentleness & kind persuasion over brute force	kindness	excess	√	
The Oak & the Reed			Yield when it is folly to resist, or be destroyed	flexibility	rigidity		tensile strength
The Old Lion & the Fox	√		Take warning from the misfortune of others	alertness	deception	√	
The Peacock	√		Don't give up freedom for looks	freedom	vanity	√	gravity
The Rooster & the Jewel	√		Sustenance is more valued than glamour	prudence			
The Wolf & his Shadow	√		Don't let your imagination make you forget reality	prudence	self deception	√	shadows

- Information on ordering Main Lesson books (page 18)

Two great sources to obtain Main Lesson books are through:
- Mercurius-USA.
- Paper, Scissors, Stone

You might also enjoy making your own book by binding together blank pages with stitches or staples. Or, just purchase a sketch pad and glue a sheet of colored paper over the cover.

- Information on how to order block crayons (page 21)

These sets of the 3 beeswax crayons in the primary colors (carmine red, ultramarine blue and lemon yellow) are handy when working with young children who are learning to create the whole rainbow of colors from just the three primary colors.

You can order these online from *Teach Wonderment* at http://shop.teachwonderment.com/Drawing-Supplies_c3.htm

- Information on ordering modeling wax and other supplies (page 23)

A great place for purchasing modeling wax and other supplies is through:
Mercurius-USA

- **Play Dough Recipe** (page 24)

Here is a simple recipe to make play dough. This can be used as an alternative modeling medium to beeswax or earth clay.
> 1 cup flour
> 1 cup warm water
> 2 teaspoons cream of tartar
> 1 teaspoon oil
> 1/4 cup salt
>
> Optional
> food coloring, cinnamon or natural scent

Mix all ingredients, adding food coloring, scent or cinnamon last.
Stir over medium heat until smooth.
Remove from pan and knead until blended smooth.
Place in plastic bag or airtight container when cooled. This will last for a long time.

♦ Instructions for making a Bee Puppet (page 46)

Making these bees can be a fun and easy craft activity. Besides being used as puppets perhaps the bees can inspire other kinds of creative play.

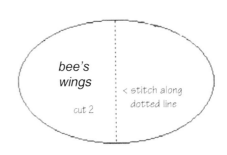

bee's wings

cut 2

< stitch along dotted line

Materials that you will need include:

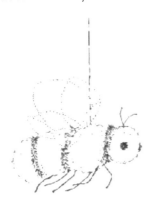

- ○ small amount of yellow lamb's wool or 2' yellow bulky spun yarn You can also use cotton wool (dye real cotton wool, not synthetic in a bowl with turmeric or a very small amount bright yellow Rit™ dye)
- ○ ½ brown chenille stem (pipe cleaner)= 6"
- ○ 1" by 4" piece of white Sparkle™ organdy, purchase the smallest amount allowed, usually 1/8yd, or use iridescent cellophane
- ○ white thread, black embroidery floss
- ○ fabric scissors, embroidery needle

Instructions: Read each step through carefully

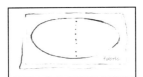

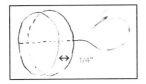

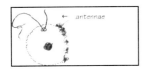

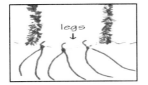

1. With fingers, work the lamb's wool or cotton wool into a smooth 1 ½" to 2" egg shape. If you are using yarn, wrap the yarn around 2 fingers 3-4 times.
2. Wrap the chenille stem (pipe cleaner) 3 times around the wool in a spiral. Bend the sharp ends of stem into the wool.
3. Fold the wing material in half and place over the wing pattern.
4. Trace the pattern onto the fabric with a soft pencil.
5. Hold the folded fabric over a light colored surface to easily see the shape marked on the fabric. Carefully cut out the two wings.
6. Thread a sewing needle with white thread (single strand).
7. Slip the top wing ¼" to the side of the other &, sew tiny running stitches, both layers together, across the center at the stitch line.
8. Gather the wing material and make an anchor stitch.
9. With the needle still threaded, stitch wings firmly to the back center of the bee. Use the remaining thread to suspend the bee.
10. Thread an embroidery needle with black embroidery floss, again single strand (usually 6 fine threads). Make several stitches on either side of the head for the bee's eyes.
11. OPTIONAL: to make the antennae, stitch, with single strand of black floss, into the top of the head. Do not pull thread all the way through. Tie the threads together and trim to ¾" length. To make legs, take a stitch as you did for the antennae, in the lower middle part of the bee, knot and cut. Repeat 2 more times to form 6 legs.

Bibliography

There are not many books listed here, but if you are teaching the fables these few can be so helpful that you should know about them.

This first book listed is one of the best basic collection of Aesop's fables. It has almost one hundred fables to choose from and, as this is a reprint of an old book, the illustrations are charming. The images could easily be adapted and simplified to serve as inspirations for your own crayon drawings or paintings. If you are unable to find it elsewhere, it is easily available online.

The Aesop for Children, with pictures by Milo Winter
Scholastic Inc.
Reprint from 1919, Checkerboard Press
ISBN 0590479776

♦ ♦ ♦ ♦ ♦ ♦ ♦ ♦ ♦ ♦ ♦ ♦ ♦ ♦ ♦ ♦

Although, to the author's mind, coloring books offer little to inspire creativity, this book is a charming resource. The illustrations were taken from a fable book from Ulm, Germany in 1476, and are unusual in that many of them show two different scenes from the same story in one image. The pictures are clearly medieval, almost childlike. Certainly you will not want to draw these outlined pictures, as they are, but adapt them to the impressionistic style of block crayons, or water colors.

Aesop's Fables, Coloring Book
Dover Publications
ISBN 048620405

♦ ♦ ♦ ♦ ♦ ♦ ♦ ♦ ♦ ♦ ♦ ♦ ♦ ♦ ♦ ♦

This is the most delightful version of *The Lion and the Mouse* I have seen yet. And even though the illustrations are in black and white, they are most beautiful. This book is well worth looking for.

The Lion and the Mouse, an Aesop's Fable
Retold by A. J. Wood,
Illustrated by Ian Andrew
The Millbrook Press
ISBN 1562946587

♦ ♦ ♦ ♦ ♦ ♦ ♦ ♦ ♦ ♦ ♦ ♦ ♦ ♦ ♦ ♦

This book is humbly included as it is a thorough guide to coloring with block crayons, one of the chief mediums for rendering illustrations of the fables. This book is available through:
TeachWonderment.com

Coloring with Block Crayons, with an emphasis on the primary colors
Sieglinde De Francesca
Teach Wonderment
ISBN 978-1-60402-996-3

Index

Color Illustrations

^   Author's block crayon drawing of *The Lion and the Mouse* to use as a guide for a child to copy.

^   A guided version of author's image by Starry Wyrzykowski (7 years old)

59

^   Wet-on-wet painting of *The Lion and the Mouse*

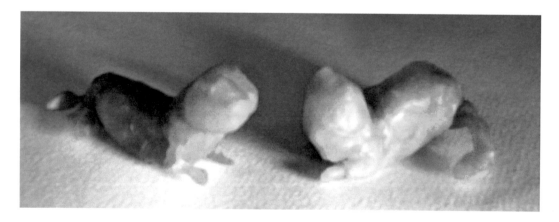

^   Beeswax lions created by second graders

^   Block crayon drawing of *The Bear and the Bees*

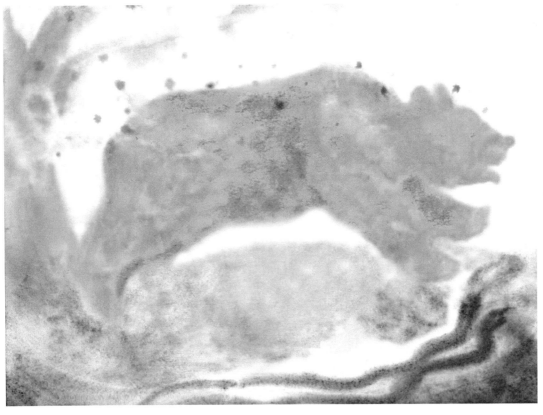

^   Water color painting of *The Bear and the Bees*

^   Block crayon drawing of *The Crow and the Pitcher*

^   Water color painting of *The Crow and the Pitcher*

^   Block crayon drawing of *The Hare and the Tortoise*
Tortoise is drawn in the "negative."

^   Water color painting of Aesop's *The Peacock*